DISNEY'S 101 DALMATIANS

Adapted from the film by Anne Mazer
Based on the motion picture from
Walt Disney Pictures

Scholastic Children's Books,
Commonwealth House, 1-19 New Oxford Street, London WC1A 1NU
A division of Scholastic Ltd
London ~ New York ~ Toronto ~ Sydney ~ Auckland

First published by Disney Press, 1996
This edition published by Scholastic Ltd, 1996

ISBN 0 590 19348 1

Typeset in Plantin by Contour Typesetters, Southall, London
Printed by Cox & Wyman Ltd, Reading, Berkshire

10 9 8 7 6 5 4 3 2 1

Contents

1

Endangered Species

Under a full yellow moon, a tiger perched majestically on top of an outcrop of rock. It was alone, the ruler of its domain. As it surveyed its territory, a twig snapped in the dense vegetation behind it.

A pale, gaunt man, dressed in a black coat, black hat and black glasses, stepped out of the bushes. As he knelt to open his rucksack, the moon lit up an ugly scar on his neck.

Lionel Skinner pulled out a rifle equipped with silencer and scope. As the tiger scanned for the enemy he sensed rather than saw, Skinner focussed on the animal's unusual black and white stripes.

With a faint, muffled pop, the rifle fired. The tiger staggered back, then tumbled off the rock.

Skinner abseiled down the rock to where the tiger's lifeless body lay. With his boot, he prodded the animal's stomach, then kneeled and took a black wooden box out of his pack. Inside it lay the instruments of the fur trade. Picking up a long, slender knife, Skinner began his grim work.

He had to work quickly, for he was not in the wild. Skinner had killed an inhabitant of London Zoo, and it was only a matter of time before its keepers arrived.

In a London bedroom, on a quiet residential street, an alarm clock was ringing loudly. The man in the bed slept through it, as did the Dalmatian on the floor. The old wind-up clock continued to ring until it tumbled off the edge of the nightstand, bumped the sleeping dog's head, and landed on the floor with a thud. The ringing stopped.

Pongo, a handsome male Dalmatian, sat up, his paws on his aching head. He staggered into the bathroom, and with his paw, turned the handle of the shower. Water shot out of the nozzle. Then he trotted back to the bedroom, took the bed sheets in his mouth, and pulled them off his sleeping owner, Roger.

Roger's nose twitched and he ground his teeth together. Pongo barked once, loudly. Roger's eyes popped open.

In the kitchen, Pongo rose up on his hind legs to the counter, and pushed the "on" switch of the coffee maker with his nose. As fresh coffee streamed into the pot, he trotted to the front door and pressed a button with his paw. The door opened and he stepped out on the porch to pick up a bottle of milk.

In another London flat, the TV news blared from the screen: ". . . of endangered animals in the wild, but never before has an animal in *captivity* been slaughtered for its pelt."

In front of the screen, Perdy, a ravishing female Dalmatian, growled and barked angrily.

"Isn't that horrible? Who could do a thing like that?" Anita, Perdy's human, came in from the kitchen, a cup of tea in her hand. She was a slender, lovely young woman in her late twenties.

Perdy whimpered in agreement.

"If the battle to preserve threatened species has moved into the urban zoological park," the reporter continued, "we must ask ourselves if any animal in the world is safe."

A frightened Perdy edged away from the TV screen.

Roger sat on a park bench and read the grim headlines, "ZOO CAT LOSES STRIPES."

"Another bad day for the animal kingdom," Roger sighed. He rolled up the paper and shoved it under his arm. "I have to get ready for my meeting this afternoon," he said to Pongo. "One day very soon, I'm going to make a sale."

He rose from the bench and picked up Pongo's lead. "We're fast approaching the point where I'm going to have to start eating your table scraps."

Pongo growled in disapproval.

"I'm exaggerating," Roger said. "It's not that bad, but it is important that the meeting goes well and you know how I am about meetings. I tend to get a little nervous . . ."

2
The House of de Vil

At the House of de Vil, the well-known fashion house, a doorman came smartly down the steps. "Top of the morning," he said as he opened the door to the white Panther de Vil limousine.

A smouldering cigarette in a long holder emerged from the car. With a single tap, an elegant finger knocked off the ash, squarely on the toe of the doorman's newly shined shoes.

A trail of cigarette smoke wafted through the black and white lobby, where another doorman stood rigidly to attention. The lift doors opened and closed, revealing walls painted in black and white tiger stripes. The man in the lift tried not to cough as the cigarette smoke enveloped him.

In the design studio, Anita bent over her drawing board, sketching a new design for the House of de Vil. The theme was tiger stripes – all the mannequins in the showroom were dressed in black and white striped garments in different stages of construction.

"Anita, darling." A cigarette burning in a long holder dangled from the elegant hand of Cruella de Vil. The owner of the House of de Vil was a striking woman with a glacial expression in her eyes. She wore a white fur over a black dress, and her hair was white-blonde on one side, and jet black on the other.

"Good morning, Cruella," Anita answered.

Cruella glanced down at Anita's drawing board. On it was a flattering sketch of Cruella in a spotted gown.

Nervously, Anita slid the drawing under another of the same gown in tiger stripes. Cruella studied it for a moment, then reached forward and moved it aside so that the two drawings were side-by-side. Then her eyes shifted to the top of the drawing board, where Anita had taped a photo of Perdy to the top corner.

Cruella picked it up. "What a charming dog."

"Thank you," Anita said.

"Spots," Cruella observed.

Behind them, the showroom was silent.

"Yes, she's a Dalmatian."

"Inspiration?" Cruella gestured to the spotted gown.

Anita's heart was pounding, but she answered calmly. "Yes."

"Long hair or short hair?"

"Short."

"Coarse or fine?"

6

"I guess I'd have to say it's a little coarse."

"Pity," Cruella drawled.

"It was very fine when she was a puppy."

"Redemption." With a smile, Cruella returned the photo to the drawing board. "We need to talk."

The doors to the design studio opened. "Ms de Vil!" Frederick, one of the company's executives, dressed all in black, bustled into the room.

"Come in to my office," Cruella told Anita, then hurried off.

As the other designers gazed at Anita in sympathy, she rolled up the drawing, took a deep breath, and rushed after them.

"Lady Ashwell called, desperate for something to wear to meet the American President," Frederick was saying as Anita caught up with them. "You'll recall that she's the rather large woman you had dinner with in December."

"You're being kind," Cruella snapped. "She's enormous. I sat in her shadow all night. Tell her she doesn't need a designer; she needs an up-holsterer."

A seamstress ran up and offered Cruella a handful of satin swatches. "It's for the lining for the gaberdine trousers."

Without slowing her pace, Cruella tested the fabric, and chose one.

"Alexandra Eaten says she doesn't want to model

your clothes any more," Frederick continued breathlessly. "She thinks they make her look short, fat and old."

Cruella shoved the swatches back at the seamstress. "She had the same complaint when she was tall, thin and young."

The three arrived at Cruella's office. Her secretary, Alonzo, held open the door. "Tea for me, Alonzo," she ordered, as she swept past him into the office.

It was an enormous black and white room, which commanded a stunning view of London. The couches were in white leather, with black cushions; and the desk, like Cruella's hair, was half-black, half-white.

Cruella shed her fur into the arms of her young assistant. "Tell me more about these spots," she said, turning to Anita. "I did leopard spots in the '80s."

"Dalmatian spots are a little different, aren't they?"

"Cosy," Cruella said.

"Cuddly," Anita echoed.

"Classic."

"Less trashy."

"Exactly," Cruella agreed. "Do you like spots, Frederick?"

"I don't believe so, madam," Frederick stammered. "I thought we liked stripes this year."

"What kind of 'yes-man' are you?" Cruella demanded.

8

Frederick passed a plump hand over his perspiring brow. "What kind of 'yes-man' would you like me to be?"

Cruella ignored him. "Frederick, I'm seeing spots now. What will it cost us to start again on next year's line?"

He shook his head. "Millions."

"Can we afford it?"

"Yes, but. . ."

"Thank you, darling," Cruella said. "Now go away. I have to talk to Anita." She crossed over to her desk and looked at some papers. "Alonzo!" she called imperiously, as he came in with the tea. "Did you ask Anita if she'd like something to drink?"

Alonzo gave Anita a panic-stricken look.

"I'm fine, thank you," Anita said hastily. She didn't want him getting in to trouble on her account.

"Sit down, please," Cruella ordered her.

Anita perched nervously on the edge of a black leather chair.

"How long have you been working for me?" Cruella asked.

She thought for a moment. "Two years last August."

"You've done wonderful work in that time."

Anita brightened at the unexpected compliment. "Thank you."

"I don't see you socially, do I?"

9

"No."

Cruella leaned back in her chair and studied Anita. "And you're not very well known, despite your obvious talent."

Anita shrugged. "Fame doesn't mean very much to me."

"Until you get a better offer," Cruella said knowingly. "Then we'll see the real Anita."

"I'm happy doing what I'm doing, thank you."

"Your work is fresh and clean, unfettered, unpretentious. It sells. And one of these days, my competitors are going to work out who you are and they're going to try and steal you away."

Anita sat up straighter. "It never occurred to me to leave my job. For another, anyway."

"What do you mean, 'anyway'?" Cruella said quickly.

"I mean that if I left, it wouldn't be for another job."

"What would it be for?"

"I don't know," Anita said slowly. "If I met someone. If working here didn't fit into our plans."

"Marriage?"

"Perhaps," Anita admitted.

"More good women have been lost to marriage than to war, famine, disease and disaster. You have talent, darling. Don't squander it."

"I don't think this is something you need to worry

about. It's not on the cards," Anita said.

"I'm really not surprised."

Anita rose. "I should get back to work."

"Why don't you come to dinner on Friday night?" Cruella asked. "We can discuss this further."

"I don't like to leave my dog alone in the evening," Anita said. "She's by herself all day."

Cruella stared at her incredulously. "You'd rather have dinner with a dog?"

"It's not a matter of what I'd *rather* do," Anita tried to explain. "It's more a matter of what I *have* to do."

Cruella snapped her fingers at Alonzo. "The drawing," she commanded.

Alonzo looked confused.

"Take the drawing from Anita and hand it to me," Cruella snapped. "Is that difficult?"

Alonzo quickly took the drawing from Anita and rushed it over to Cruella. "Thank you," Cruella drawled. "Go and stand somewhere until I need you."

Her assistant scurried to a far corner and stood stiffly at attention.

Cruella opened the drawing. "I look wonderful in spots," she murmured. "However, I would like to make one small change." She plucked a pen from the inkwell, and frowning intently, began to rework it.

Anita craned her neck, trying to see what Cruella

11

was doing. "We could do this in linen," she suggested.

"We could do it in any number of materials. It's never the material. It's the pattern." Cruella finished the drawing, then put down her pen and leaned back with a smile. She held the drawing out, then looked at Alonzo and rattled it impatiently. He scurried to the desk to take the drawing, and then stood there, waiting for orders.

"Give it to Anita," Cruella ordered.

"Thank you." He hurried to Anita, then looked back at Cruella. "Wait in the corner?"

"Please," Cruella said.

Anita studied the drawing. Cruella had changed the dress into an elegant ankle-length coat. She gazed at her boss in admiration. What talent she had!

Anita laughed to herself. "This is rather funny." She carefully rolled up the drawing.

"What's that, darling?"

"If we make this coat," Anita said slowly, "it'll be like you're wearing my dog."

Cruella laughed, and her evil laughter continued long after Anita left her office.

3
Love at First Sight

Roger sat in front of a large, elegant desk, explaining the latest video game and feeling more nervous every minute. "It's a work in progress," he apologized. "The graphics are very rough."

Behind the desk, a young man nodded in a friendly way to Roger while sipping water from a bottle.

With a burst of renewed confidence, Roger continued his pitch. "Normally, I'd finish the game completely, then bring it to you, but. . ." He paused. "I need the money. I'm freelancing now. Without a regular salary, money's a little tight."

Allan nodded politely. "I'm not the one you have to convince."

The two men got up and Allan led the way to a back room, where a small, pale nine year old was playing Roger's video game with savage concentration.

On screen, a red ball sailed into a forest. "Fetch!" commanded a voice. An animated Dalmatian

13

bounded after the ball.

Roger and Allan stood in the doorway and watched the kid play. "Herbert's got the best instincts in the industry," Allan explained. "Since he was six, he's picked the top-selling game every year."

Herbert let out a rapid succession of joystick shots. At a final bark from the Dalmatian, he leaned back from the monitor.

"What do you think?" Roger asked him eagerly.

He hopped out of the chair and walked over to Roger. "Potentially good graphics, reasonably entertaining idea, the dog's well conceived, the environments are engaging," the kid, who barely reached Roger's waist, rattled off.

Roger broke into a grin.

"But I'm not interested in a game that has a chubby little dog catcher as the bad guy," Herbert continued. "Am I a hero because I outrun an overweight government worker?"

He slung a rucksack over his shoulder. "Even girls won't like this," he concluded. "Sorry, mate."

"What if it had a better villain?" Roger cried. He *had* to make a success of this game. "Someone you'd really hate."

"It's not hatred that's important," Herbert informed him. "It's a desire to annihilate."

Tethered to a bicycle rack, Pongo waited patiently for Roger to come out of his meeting. He wasn't bored, though. There were always dogs and people to watch. A bicycle came down the street, leading an attractive Dalmatian on a lead. Pongo stared after her, his mouth open. He had never seen such a beautiful dog.

The other dog turned towards him, and for a moment, their eyes met. A shiver ran through Pongo. He strained forward on his lead, barking madly.

"Sorry, Pongo." It was Roger, sounding tired and dejected. "I didn't know I was going to take so long."

Pongo kept barking. The Dalmatian and her owner were heading down the street. He couldn't lose them.

"Calm down, boy." Roger unlocked his bike. "If I could sell a game, we might be able to get a car," he said wistfully.

Still barking wildly, Pongo ran alongside Roger's bike, his lead attached to the handlebars.

"Pongo! What's the matter with you?" Roger tried to turn right, but Pongo veered left, towing the bike and Roger after him. "PONGO!"

They shot down a street, narrowly missing several pedestrians, and causing several cars to slam on their brakes.

"PONGO!" Roger squeezed the brakes, but they didn't hold. The bike swerved round a corner, and

15

into an arcade, scattering shoppers before them. Then Pongo bounded down a flight of stairs, the bike bumping violently behind him.

"PONGO! STOP!" Roger screamed, as they raced into a crowded junction and alongside a large red double-decker bus.

Ahead of them, Anita and Perdy turned into St. James's Park. As Pongo galloped in frantic pursuit, a military band marched towards them in precise formation. Roger cried out in terror.

Just in time, the soldiers stepped aside. The bike and dog sped past.

The lead ring holding Pongo to the bike strained and then snapped. Pongo sped after Perdy, while Roger and the bike flew out of control in the opposite direction.

Roger screamed as the bike hurtled across a lawn and slammed into a bench. He tumbled off, sailed through the air, and landed with a tremendous splash in the middle of a duck pond.

A little later, a wet and bedraggled Roger rode his bicycle slowly out of the park. His jumper hung to his knees; one shoe was missing; his flannel trousers drooped and sagged. The bike had not fared much better. The frame was twisted into a V. It wobbled and squeaked as he rode it. "PONGO?!" he yelled. He couldn't wait until he got his hands on that dog.

Suddenly he saw him. Pongo was bounding after a ball thrown by an attractive young woman. Roger slowed to a halt and crept after him. Then he leapt. "I've got you now!" Roger cried.

Anita gasped as Roger holding on to Perdy's collar, stood up, and dragged her towards his bicycle.

"LET GO OF THAT DOG!" she yelled.

Roger's mouth was set in a thin line. "Stay out of this, lady."

"Stop, or I'll . . . I'll hit you."

"Today is not a good day to threaten me, ma'am."

Anita glared at him. "I don't care if it's a good day or a bad day . . . I'll hit you anyway."

"Whatever," Roger said with a shrug. First the video game, then the bike chase, now this crazy lady.

She pulled her shoulder bag off her arm. "I gave you a proper warning," she said.

Roger sighed. "I've had just about . . ."

She swung, hitting him hard on the head. He went down. "Release my dog or I'll hit you again," she threatened.

Puzzled and groggy, Roger stared at Anita. "*Your* dog?"

She nodded. "That's my dog. Let her go."

Roger looked closely at Perdy. "He's a *she*," he said, finally understanding. A familiar canine face peeked out from behind Anita's legs and whimpered.

"Hello, Pongo," Roger said grimly. He released Perdy and stood up. "I beg your pardon, ma'am."

As he put Pongo on his lead, he turned to Anita and asked, "What do you have in that handbag of yours? Rocks?"

"Bricks. I'm paving my garden and every time I see a discarded brick, I pick it up."

"Oh yes," Roger said. "How many did you find today?"

"Three."

"That's what I would have guessed." He gingerly rubbed the back of his head.

Anita stared at his soggy jumper and dripping trousers. "Why are you all wet?"

"I went swimming in the pond," he said sarcastically.

"The water's filthy," she pointed out.

"And it tastes like fish."

"You fell in, didn't you?" she said. "No one with their wits about them swims in a dirty pond in their nice jumper and trousers. And you've lost a shoe. Did you know that?"

"As a matter of fact, I did. I noticed it running down the *gravel* path."

"I'm ever so sorry," she snapped back. "I thought that perhaps if you were silly enough to swim in a pond, you'd be silly enough not to know you'd lost a shoe."

18

"I crashed my bicycle in the pond," Roger said wearily. "The only part of my body that wasn't injured was my head. But now, thanks to you, I have the complete set of bodily injuries." He held out his hand. "It was nice being assaulted by you, Ms . . .?"

"My name's Anita and yours is Roger." She took his hand and shook it. "I read your dog's identification tag."

"Nice to meet you. I'm very sorry if I alarmed you."

"It's understandable since we both seem to have a certain fondness for Dalmatians," Anita smiled at him.

"And they clearly have a certain fondness for each other."

They gazed down at the two dogs sitting close together.

Roger tugged at Pongo's lead. "Your roving eye has caused me enough trouble today, Pongo," he said. "Let's go home."

"Are you going to be all right? Perhaps you should call your doctor," Anita said anxiously.

"Good luck with your bricks." Roger started down the path.

"If you have concussion, you shouldn't be alone."

Roger ignored her. All he wanted to do was get home and into some dry clothes.

"Do you have someone who can keep an eye on you?" she called after him.

As he disappeared down the path, Anita looked down at Perdy. "He's a jolly nice human, don't you think?"

Perdy barked in agreement.

Roger wheeled his bike towards home. "You could have got me killed, Pongo," he said sternly. "You risked losing your master for a brief frolic with a female."

Pongo hung his head.

"Fools aren't born, Pongo," he lectured. "Pretty girls make them in their spare time." Roger got on his wrecked bicycle, making sure to keep the lead clear.

Pongo looked round for Perdy. She was trotting next to Anita's bike. The two dogs barked longingly at each other.

"Don't even think about it," Roger warned.

When they got to the Victoria Monument, Roger paused and looked back. Anita and Perdy were coming down Constitution Hill. Their eyes met for a moment, then Roger quickly turned away and began to pedal in the other direction. He wasn't going to make a fool of himself like Pongo.

As Anita approached the monument, Roger decided to take another turn round it. Pongo looked up at his master and barked in approval.

"You have it entirely wrong, Pongo," Roger said. "I'm simply trying to decide on a route home. It has nothing . . ." He blinked as the sun blinded him momentarily. When he opened his eyes, Anita was gone. ". . . nothing whatever to do with Anita. If that's what her name is." He turned towards home.

Pongo craned his head toward the Monument and barked loudly. From somewhere nearby, Perdy responded.

"PERDY! STOP!" Anita shrieked.

Roger jumped off his bike and stared, open-mouthed, as Perdy towed Anita's bike at high speed in the direction of the pond.

"LOOK OUT!" he yelled, running after them, but it was too late.

4
A Wedding

An ice bag on his head, a mug of tea in his hands, and a blanket around his shoulders, Roger sat in front of a roaring fire in his living-room. Next to him, under another blanket, sat Anita. "I've never been rescued before," she said, cradling a hot mug of tea in her hands. "It was very exciting. And you were ever so sweet to give me a kiss."

"Thank you." There was another silence. Anita sipped at her tea, and Roger gazed at the two dogs, who sat beneath a blanket in front of the fire. "I think we have a problem," he finally said. "I think my dog's in love."

"I think mine is, too," Anita agreed. She turned to look at him. "Why is that a problem?"

"They're going to be broken-hearted when you leave."

The two dogs gazed plaintively at their owners.

"I don't think I can bear to live with a broken-hearted Dalmatian," Anita said softly.

22

"They're miserable when they're lonely," Roger agreed.

Anita put her cup down. "We'd better think of something."

"I agree. Would you like another cup of marriage?"

"Excuse me?" Anita couldn't believe her ears.

"Tea. Another cup of tea?"

"You said *marriage*," Anita pointed out.

"Marriage?" Roger shifted uncomfortably on the couch.

"That's what you said. You meant to say tea, but it came out as marriage." She smiled at him.

"I'm sorry. Do you want another cup of tea?"

"I do," Anita said.

"You do?"

"I will."

"You will?"

"If you ask me."

Roger gazed nervously into his tea cup. "Would you . . .?"

"Yes," Anita answered.

Their eyes met. Slowly, they moved closer until they kissed.

Close to the fire, Pongo and Perdy snuggled happily together.

Anita and Roger faced each other at the altar, their hands joined.

23

"God bless, preserve and keep you," the minister intoned.

With a subtle shift of his eyes, Roger signalled Anita to look towards the open church doors.

Anita followed the direction of his glance. There stood Pongo and Perdy.

In honour of the occasion, Pongo wore a black silk rope collar with a silver clasp, while Perdy wore a white silk and lace cord collar with a silver heart-shaped clasp. ". . . and so fill you with all spiritual benediction and grace . . ." The two dogs bowed their heads.

Anita and Roger smiled at each other. "Amen," concluded the minister.

Roger lifted Anita's veil and kissed her. Pongo and Perdy wagged their tails. Church bells rang. Outside the church, hundreds of dogs gathered on the steps broke into a thunderous chorus of barks, yelps and yips heard over the entire city of London.

5

Jasper and Horace

I ts tailpipe belching clouds of grey odorous smoke, the old truck rattled round the corner, and pulled to a wheezing stop.

"What's the address?" Jasper hunched over the wheel and peered out the window. He was a tall, gaunt man with bushy eyebrows and small darting eyes.

"It's slipped my mind, Jasper." Horace was short on height and brainpower. His nose was fat, his brain was dull; he hadn't shaved in days.

"You don't have *any* idea what the number might be?"

Horace struggled to think. "No."

Jasper reached down, grabbed a monkey wrench, and conked him on the head.

"152 Merton Road, London SW1 9EH, red brick townhouse with a black door," Horace recited rapidly. "You need the telephone number?"

A few minutes later, they were in front of the door.

"Let me tell you about this bloke, Skinner, before

25

we meet him," Jasper warned in a low voice. "When he was quite young, a dog tore open his throat and damaged his vocal chords leaving him brutally scarred and completely mute. He can't talk at all."

He lifted the door knocker and let it fall. The thud resounded through the street. "Pay attention," Jasper said sharply. "This is important. Two things you mustn't do. One. Don't look at the scar on his neck. Two. Don't talk to him."

"Right," said Horace brightly.

The door creaked open. Horace's eyes bulged and his mouth dropped open. "Oh! Look at the size of that scar! No wonder you can't talk!"

Skinner's eyes narrowed, and a muscle in his jaw pulsed. Automatically, his hand reached up to touch the scar.

Jasper yanked Horace into a room. "Won't be a minute," he apologized to Skinner. He slammed the door shut. From behind it came the sound of a loud slap.

Skinner's tannery was crammed with pelts of all kinds, stuffed and mounted animals and birds. The room reeked of dried blood. Knives and other tools of the fur trade lay on the tables.

"Bloody gruesome line of work you're in, Skinner," Jasper said approvingly.

Horace shuddered. With a ferocious scowl, Skinner

26

took out a black leather case and thrust it into Jasper's arms.

"Much obliged, sunshine," Jasper said cheerily.

Horace tipped his hat to Skinner, who stared fixedly at his uncovered head. "What?" he asked.

"I think he'd like to turn your mop into a tea cosy."

Slowly, Horace backed away from Skinner's weird gaze. The guy was creepy. But Jasper was laughing as if it were a joke.

Out of the truck, Jasper tossed the case on the seat. On its side, a bright sticker proclaimed, "I ♥ London Zoo."

In her sumptuous bedroom, Cruella sat in bed with a breakfast tray, her correspondence and the morning paper. As she scanned the society pages, her eyes suddenly narrowed. "How could she do this to me?" she burst out furiously.

She took one more look at the wedding picture of Roger and Anita, Pongo and Perdy, then crumpled up the newspaper and tossed it angrily onto the floor.

Alonzo poked his head into the room. "The gentlemen are here."

"Send them in," Cruella ordered, then added nastily, "and sort your hair out."

"Morning, ma'am." Jasper said respectfully. He carried the black leather case under one arm. Horace

27

followed him, his mouth hanging open at the opulence of the room.

Cruella waved Alonzo away.

"Lovely day, madam," Jasper said. "Blue skies, birds singing, the laughter of children. It's the kind of day when there wouldn't be an unhappy face in all of London."

"There is one and I'm wearing it," Cruella snapped.

"Fortunately, there's a wicked storm coming in off the Atlantic . . ." Jasper quickly amended. He patted the case resting on his knees. "I have a little present from Mr Skinner."

He crossed over to the bed and opened the case. Inside lay the pelt of the tiger Skinner had shot at the zoo.

Cruella's anger disappeared as she pulled the black and white fur out of the case. "It's magnificent," she breathed.

She rose with it in her arms and slid it over her shoulders.

"Siberian Tiger suits madam very well," Jasper said.

With the fur over her shoulders, Cruella crossed to her dressing room.

"Notice, Horace," Jasper said loudly, "how the black and white of the wild beast pays homage to madam's own hairstyle." He hoped Cruella would hear him.

Above: Pongo gently wakes Roger.

Below: In hot pursuit of Perdy, Pongo pulls a terrified Roger along the city streets.

Above: Pongo and Perdy meet in the park at last – and so do Anita and Roger!

Below: Hands joined, the happy couple stands at the altar.

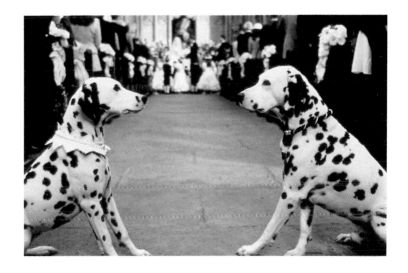

Above: Just down the aisle, Pongo and Perdy take their vows as well.

Below: A canine wedding party celebrates Pongo and Perdy's marriage with a chorus of barks, howls and yelps

Above: Cruella is extremely pleased with Jasper's furry gift.

Below: A bed only Cruella could love!

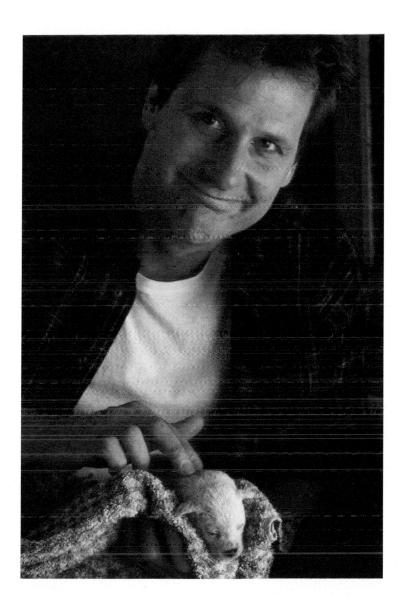

Above: After a close call, Roger smiles and strokes Lucky's tiny head.

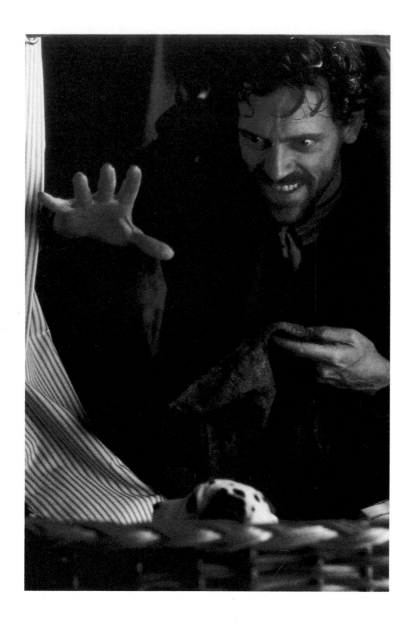

Above: Jasper greedily plucks the last frightened pup from the bed.

Above: Kipper nudges the puppies out of Cruella's library and away from danger.

Below: Fogey keeps a careful eye on the puppies hidden beneath the fluffy sheep.

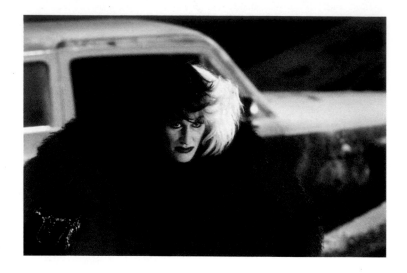

Above: Cruella steps out of the Panther De Vil, demanding to know the whereabouts of the ninety-nine puppies.

Below: The squirrels outsmart the bungling duo once again, and Horace ends up black in the face!

Horace tugged at his tea cup. He had his finger stuck in the handle.

In the dressing room, Cruella modelled the fur before a full-length mirror. Closing her eyes, she stroked it against her face.

Jasper watched in alarm as Horace struggled with the tea cup. "Grip it, twist and yank!" he yelled.

In the other room, Cruella's eyes snapped open. "What?!"

Jasper laughed apologetically. "Just recommending a law firm to my associate here. He's currently with . . ." He glared at Horace. "Hold it, wiggle, and tug."

Horace held the cup with one hand and yanked with the other. His finger popped out. As Jasper watched in horror, the cup slipped from Horace's other hand and flew into the air.

The cup *pinged* against the ceiling and fell. Horace held out his hat and caught it neatly. The two of them stood frozen as Cruella entered the bedroom.

"What's wrong with you?" Cruella demanded in a harsh voice.

Jasper stared at her. "Nothing."

"Nothing," Horace echoed stupidly.

"You didn't think I was going to pay you." She smiled nastily and headed towards her desk.

Silently, Horace took the cup from his hat, tiptoed over to the tea trolley and replaced it.

29

Cruella grabbed an envelope full of cash from her desk and pulled out a thick wad of notes. The two men exchanged satisfied glances.

"Go back to your hovel and wait until I need you again," she commanded.

"I thank you for your continued patronage." Jasper gestured at Horace, who leaned nervously on the tea cart. "As does my associate."

"I do indeed," Horace said, trying to match Jasper in flowery language. "And might I add that you serve a very lovely . . ." He leaned forward for emphasis. ". . . cup of . . ."

Unbalanced by his weight, the tea cart flipped on its back wheels. Horace fell forward, the tea service hurled backwards, and tea cups and saucers shattered against the wall.

Cruella's eyes glittered with anger. She thrust out her open palm. Jasper slowly put the money back in her hand.

"We'll be at the hovel," he said sadly, as he and Horace slunk out of the room.

6

More to Come

In her new living room, Anita hung a picture on the wall, while Nanny, the housekeeper, dusted the blinds, and chattered happily away. "I so loved living with your family when you were little," Nanny confided, "and now to be with you again as you start a family of your own is a dream come true."

Anita shook her head. "I'm not sure Roger and I are quite ready to start a family, Nanny."

"That's a shame. Well, first the puppies, then the babies . . ."

"Puppies?" Anita stared at her. What was Nanny talking about?

On the second floor, Roger worked on his video game. "If I've done my job right, when this new villain comes on, you're going to run from the room in a panic," he told Pongo.

Pongo's ears pricked up as he watched the screen. An animated Dalmatian ran into a hollow log.

Suddenly an evil, slime-dripping dog catcher, brandishing a net, appeared onscreen.

Roger turned to Pongo, expecting him to bolt in terror. Instead, Pongo yawned. With a sigh of defeat, Roger flipped off the control.

"It's unmistakable, dear," Nanny said to Anita. She pared an apple and put it in a big blue bowl. "You can see it, can't you?"

Anita studied Perdy intently, but she couldn't see anything different about her. Well, she did look unusually contented and happy.

"It's the look every woman gets when she knows she is going to be a mother," Nanny explained. "Notice how tranquil she is? Her eyes are soft and warm."

Unknowingly, Anita's face took on the same expression.

"And though you might not see it," Nanny continued, "you can certainly feel that she's smiling. It's the smile we wear when we're guarding a precious secret."

A quiet smile flitted across Anita's face.

"Now she's living for others as well as herself. She's eating more."

As if in response to Nanny's words, Anita bit into an apple slice and sighed. Then she leaned over and hugged Perdy. "I think you're right, Nanny," she finally said. "She does look different."

Nanny set down the paring knife and stared as Anita took another slice of apple and smiled sleepily at her.

"What is it, Nanny?"

"Oh, goodness!" Nanny put her hand to her chest. "Anita, dear . . . I think you're going to have a puppy."

Cruella was waiting in the living room as they came back from the doctor's. "Anita! Darling!" she cried, rising dramatically from the couch.

"Cruella!"

She embraced Anita. Suddenly she caught sight of the dogs, cowering behind Roger in the hallway. Her smile faded.

The dogs barked furiously at her. Cruella smiled again. "Oh, Anita! Those dazzling dogs!" She nodded curtly to Roger. "You must be Rufus."

Roger stuck out his hand. "It's Roger and it's a pleasure, Ms de Vil."

"What's a pleasure?" she asked rudely.

"Making your acquaintance," Roger replied.

"Such a sweet thought," Cruella purred. "I wish I could reciprocate." She blew a cloud of smoke in his direction.

Ignoring his outstretched hand, she turned to Anita. "Tell me. You married him for his dog."

Anita shot a quick apologetic look towards Roger. He shooed the dogs upstairs and came into the living room.

Cruella swooped onto the sofa. "I've missed you darling. I hate the fact that you're on leave."

"I'm still working," Anita protested. "You've been getting my sketches?"

"It's not the same. I miss the interaction." She turned to Roger. "And what is it that you do that allows you to support Anita in such splendour?"

"I design video games."

"Video games?" Cruella mimicked. "Is he having me on?"

Anita sprang to Roger's defence. "No. He's very good at it. It's a growing business."

"Those horrible noisy things that children play on their televisions? Someone *designs* them? What a senseless thing to do with your life."

Roger took a deep breath and changed the subject. "Did Anita tell you the news?" he asked. "She's going to have a baby."

"Is this true?" Cruella demanded.

Anita nodded.

Cruella flicked her cigarette ash on the floor. "You poor thing. I'm so sorry."

"I'm excited about it, Cruella."

Cruella stared at her. "You can't be serious."

"She is," Roger said firmly.

"What can I say?" Cruella sighed. "Accidents will happen."

"We're having puppies, too," Roger said.

Cruella rose and took another drag on her cigarette. "I must say this is somewhat better news. I adore puppies." She turned to Anita. "I will expect a decline in your work load."

"I shouldn't think so," Anita answered.

"Be sure and let me know when the blessed event occurs."

"It won't be for another eight months."

"The *puppies*, darling." Cruella crossed to the entry and flung open the door. "I have no *use* for babies," she said.

7

Puppies and More Puppies!

On a cold rainy autumn afternoon some months later, Roger sat at the dining room table doing a crossword puzzle. Every few minutes, he glanced at the clock, then at his watch. Finally he rose and crossed to the kitchen door, then looked back at Pongo. "If I'm this nervous about your puppies, what am I going to be like when *my* baby arrives?" He plonked himself back into the chair. "How can you be so calm?"

Pongo gazed at Roger with tired eyes.

The door to the kitchen swung open and Nanny rushed out. Roger and Pongo both jumped up.

"Not yet," Nanny said, as she hurried past them.

"What's taking so long?" Roger demanded.

From somewhere upstairs, Nanny yelled, "These things take time!"

Roger sank back into the chair and tried to concentrate on his crossword puzzle. "Four letter word for 'dome. . .'"

In response, Pongo woofed softly.

"Thank you." Carefully, Roger penciled in the word "roof."

A bolt of lightning flashed through the sky and thunder rumbled, as Jasper and Horace's truck pulled up in front of Roger and Anita's house. "Go peep in the window and see if the puppies have come yet," Jasper ordered.

"It's pouring buckets, Jasper," Horace whined.

"How could I not have noticed?" Jasper said sarcastically.

"Might be because you were concentrating on your driving."

"Of course I know it's raining!" Jasper screeched. "Go and look through the window."

Horace rubbed his nose. "Have we got an umbrella?"

Reaching down between the seats, Jasper pulled out an umbrella and dumped it on Horace's lap. "Careful when you open it."

With a snap and a whoosh, the umbrella flew open. "Is it bad luck to open an umbrella in a van?" Horace asked plaintively.

In the kitchen, Anita sat on the floor next to Perdy, gently stroking her head. Suddenly, Perdy lay down.

"NANNY!" Anita cried.

Nanny rushed into the kitchen with her arms full of towels. "Gangway!" she yelled.

Horace slid out of the truck and yanked the open umbrella through the door, turning it inside out.

"Now look what you've done to my umbrella!" Jasper cried.

Horace shut and then opened it again. The ribs were bent and twisted. "It should be fine now." His mouth dropped open. "I'm sorry Jasper, I forgot what I'm supposed to do."

Jasper grabbed the monkey wrench and conked him on the head. A brief spark of intelligence flickered in Horace's eyes. "I'll go and look through the window and see if them puppies have been born yet. And . . . ?"

Jasper gave him another conk.

". . . run down to the pub and tell the missus if I see any."

"That's right," Jasper growled.

Horace looked confused again. "Why would they have puppies in the pub?"

"The house!" Jasper said. "Look through the window of the *house*!"

Horace nodded sagely. "For . . . ?"

"PUPPIES!" Jasper shrieked.

"THEY'RE HERE! THE PUPPIES ARE HERE!"

Nanny cried, as she burst into the dining room where Pongo and Roger were waiting.

"You're a father, Pongo!" Roger congratulated him.

Pongo barked joyfully.

Back in the kitchen, Nanny called out. "Two!"

"You're a father twice," Roger told Pongo.

"MAKE THAT THREE!" Nanny shouted.

Pongo threw his head back and howled with pride.

Looking in through the kitchen window, Horace broke into a grin. Then he rushed away in the direction of the pub.

An hour later, a weary but radiant Nanny appeared. "Fifteen puppies!" she announced, then vanished again into the kitchen.

Pongo stared after her in disbelief.

Roger stroked Pongo's head. "Did you hear that, boy? Fifteen puppies!"

A few minutes later, Nanny reappeared, holding a bundle in her arms. "Fourteen," she said quietly. "We lost one." She handed it to Roger.

"I'm sorry, Pongo. I'm so sorry." Roger sat down with the little bundle.

Pongo sniffed it, then nudged it with his nose. He nudged it again, and looked up at Roger.

"I wonder . . ." As Pongo watched him intently, Roger gently stroked the little puppy under the towel, then pressed and pushed on it again and again.

Suddenly there was a little wiggle under the towel. A small pink nose pushed out.

Pongo and Roger exchanged triumphant glances. Slowly, Roger unwrapped the towel to reveal a tiny alert puppy with two black ears and a black circle around one eye.

Roger rose, with the puppy clutched in his arms. "Fifteen!" he called. "We have fifteen puppies!"

Nanny rushed out from the kitchen. "Mercy! Mercy!" She took the puppy from Roger. "We're naming this one Lucky!"

Anita came into the living-room.

"How's Perdy?" Roger asked her.

"Tired." Anita didn't look too good herself. Her hair was dishevelled and there were dark circles under her eyes.

"Bringing fifteen puppies into the world. I suppose she has a right," Roger said sympathetically.

"They're so beautiful." Anita nodded to Pongo, who waited expectantly by the kitchen door. "You can go in, Pongo." She flopped down on a chair with a weary sigh. "I'm glad I'm only having one."

8

Not for Sale

A triple flash of lightning illuminated the sky as Cruella de Vil, in a black mink coat and matching hat, marched up to Anita and Roger's house, and swept through the front door.

"Anita? Anita!" she cried.

In the living room, Anita cast a frightened look at Roger and jumped to her feet.

"There you are," Cruella snapped. "Where are the puppies?"

Anita stared at her in bewilderment.

"They should have arrived by now," Cruella said impatiently.

Roger stepped forward. "Excuse me!"

Ignoring him completely, Cruella barged into the kitchen. Anita, Roger and Nanny hurried after her.

As Perdy cowered and tried to protect her babies, Pongo stood and bared his teeth.

"Those are puppies?" Cruella's lip curled in disgust. "They look like white rats."

"Their spots don't come until later," Anita explained.

"You're sure?"

"Yes."

Cruella nodded her head curtly. "All right. Put them in a bag. I'll take them with me now."

"They've just been born," Roger protested.

"I can *see* that."

"Cruella, they have to be with their mother for several weeks," Anita told her. "They're not ready to leave."

"Fine. Then put them on reserve for me." She opened her handbag and pulled out her cheque book and pen. "How much would you like?"

"They're not for sale," Roger said firmly.

"You've come into some money, have you?" Cruella said with withering scorn. "Did you design some silly game that will drive delinquent kiddies into a frenzy of video delight?"

"As a matter of fact . . ." Roger's voice was low and angry.

"We're not sure we're going to sell the puppies," Anita quickly interrupted. "That's what Roger meant to say."

"How many are there?" Cruella demanded.

Anita answered. "Fifteen."

"Fifteen times . . . five hundred pounds? Seven and-a-half thousand pounds," she concluded. "Fair?

Two pounds per spot?" Cruella opened the cheque-book and began making out the cheque.

"Why would you want fifteen puppies?" Anita asked.

"It's irrelevant, Anita," Roger said. "She can't have *any*. They're not for sale."

Cruella's eyes narrowed. "I'm getting very tired of you, Roger." She tore the cheque from the book and held it out to Anita. "Take it."

Anita looked at Roger for a clue as what to do. In her basket on the floor, Perdy whimpered with fear.

Cruella rattled the cheque. "Take it!" she ordered.

Anita took a breath. "Cruella, the puppies aren't for sale."

"You're quite sure?"

"Yes," she and Roger answered together.

Stunned, Cruella glared at them. Then she ripped the cheque into pieces and threw them in Anita's face. "You're a fool," she said furiously. "I have no use for fools. You're fired. You're finished. You'll never work in fashion again. What a pity. Enjoy your poverty, revel in your obscurity."

As she stomped from the room, Cruella turned to Roger. Her eyes glittered with a cold malice. "Remember. I had her first."

The front door slammed behind her.

9

Dognapping!

"I've got them! They're here!" Nanny came through the door, set a package wrapped in brown paper on the desk, and took off her coat. A wave of puppies cascaded down the stairs and surrounded her, yelping joyously. "To the kitchen, everyone! Anita! Roger!"

Inside the package were fifteen small boxes. Anita opened the first one. "Jewel?" she said. A small puppy with spots in the shape of necklace, stepped forward. Slowly Anita fastened a red leather dog collar around her neck. On it was a brass tag engraved with her name.

"Dipstick?" Roger called.

Then it was Nanny's turn. "Fidget?"

"Two-tone?"

Soon fourteen of the puppies were wearing new collars. Anita picked up the last collar, and looked around for its owner. Water tinkled on to the kitchen floor. A puppy peeked shamefacedly out from beneath the table.

"Wizzer," Anita and Roger sighed in unison.

"I'll get the mop," Nanny said.

From their truck, Jasper and Horace watched as Anita, Roger, Pongo, and Perdy set out on their evening walk. As soon as they were around the corner, the two thugs took off their caps, yanked black tights over their heads, and replaced the caps.

"Let's go," Jasper growled.

The two men reached for the doors, then Jasper leaned back and glared at Horace. They couldn't move – they had put the same pair of tights on their heads.

At the kitchen counter, Nanny cleaned up after the puppies, scooping the leftovers from their dishes. "Somebody didn't finish their supper," she grumbled. "We're on a budget. There's no accounting for waste."

The doorbell rang. Nanny went to the door and opened it a crack. Two men with black tights over their heads stood on the step. They tipped their caps to her. "Evening, ma'am."

With a shriek, Nanny flung herself against the door, but Jasper quickly wedged his foot in.

Horace leaned forward. "It's all right, lady," he said loudly. "We're professionals!" He winced as

Jasper elbowed him in the side to shut him up.

Frantically, Nanny tried to hold the door shut and screamed loudly, hoping someone, anyone, would hear. Suddenly the security chain broke. The two men pushed their way into the house.

From the cupboard underneath the stairs came Nanny's muffled screams. Jasper and Horace peeled off their masks and made their way to the kitchen.

"The old bird put up a good fight," Jasper said. "I admire spirit in a gal."

"Easy for you to say," Horace grumbled. "You didn't take a boot in the backside." He took the sack that Jasper held out to him.

"Hold the bag. I'll get the puppies." Jasper ripped open the curtains under the sink. The puppies huddled behind Wizzer, who growled fearlessly, then lunged and clamped his teeth on Jasper's finger.

Meanwhile Horace had spotted an uncovered dish of leftover dog food. He sniffed it, smiled and picked up a spoon.

"The bag!" Jasper shrieked. Pain did not improve his temper. Jasper tossed the puppies into it. "That's the lot," Jasper snarled. "Let's get out of here."

Horace took another bite of dog food. "Mmmm. Good."

"What is the matter with you?" asked Jasper.

"I haven't eaten since breakfast." Horace held out a spoonful to Jasper, who recoiled in disgust.

46

"What do you think this is?" he demanded.

Horace chewed thoughtfully. "I don't have to think. I know. It's paté." He scooped out the last bit and set the empty container aside. "A nice duck paté with pistachio nuts and fennel."

"You're a prat," Jasper jeered. "You're eating dog food." With a loud laugh, he swung the bag of puppies over his back and walked out of the house.

Flushed with pride, Jasper strolled down the street with the bag of whimpering puppies slung over his back.

"'Evening, Guv." He tipped his head to an older man walking a bulldog along the street.

The bulldog turned and barked ferociously at Jasper. His owner tugged on his lead. "Montgomery! Heel, boy!"

Jasper ignored the dog. He opened the back of his truck and tossed the sack of puppies in.

"You know what I think, Jasper?" Horace glanced fearfully at the barking dog. "I think that bulldog knows what we've just done."

"Dog's ain't got the mind to work things out, Horace. Chances are the mutt's just got a whiff of the horse meat on your breath." He locked the van and put his hand reassuringly on his partner's shoulder. "The downfall of the canine population is that they're too stupid to realize that there's some among us what want to do them harm."

47

The bulldog kept up his alarm. Across the park, Pongo's ears pricked up. Perdy, too, began to bark. Pulling free from Anita and Roger, the two dogs took off towards home.

"Perdy! Pongo!" Roger called after them.

Anita frowned. "Something's happened!"

At the front door, Perdy and Pongo howled to be let in. Nanny freed herself from the cupboard and rushed to open it. "Thank goodness, you're home!"

The two dogs raced to the kitchen, where they skidded to a halt. Pongo's ears dropped. Perdy nudged the empty dog basket with her nose and whimpered.

Behind them, a desolate Anita, Roger and Nanny stood in the doorway. The puppies were gone.

10

Animal Rally

When the phone rang, Cruella was lying on a sofa in her library and smoking a cigarette. Across from her, a visitor sat by the fire.

"Evening, ma'am," said Jasper on the other end of the line. "I sincerely hope I'm not disturbing your relaxation but I've got good news."

"Did you get the puppies?" At his answer, her face brightened. "All of them?" She took a long drag on her cigarette. "My faith in your limited intelligence is momentarily restored."

"You're too kind, ma'am."

Cruella hung up. "They've got the fifteen," she said to her visitor. "Anita's finally paid me back for all I've done for her. Poor thing, she'll never know how much it means to me." She laughed coldly.

Lionel Skinner took out a notebook and pen from his pocket and began to calculate. He added the fifteen to another number and wrote down the total: ninety-nine.

In the back of the truck, Wizzer wriggled and squirmed until he had forced an opening in the bag which imprisoned him and his brothers and sisters. Then he squeezed through and sniffed at the rusty hole in the back door. Was anyone out there? He gave a short, sharp bark.

A terrier named Kipper, lying in the doorway of a nearby cottage, pricked up his ears. He stumbled to his feet and barked a response. The two dogs began to communicate.

Making their way towards the truck, Jasper and Horace stumbled out of the pub with bottles in paper bags. "I'm gonna go to bed," Jasper yawned. "I'm dead tired."

Horace cocked his head. "I'm hearing dogs again, Jasper."

Jasper drew his leg back and kicked the rusting door of the truck. "Shut up in there!" he bawled. He got into the cab and started up the van.

Kipper ran after it, as fast as his short legs could carry him. But at the top of a hill he stopped, panting and exhausted. The van rumbled away and was lost in the dark, moonlit night.

The fire in Roger and Anita's living room crackled. But the two dogs who lay in front of it were listless and mournful, deeply worried about the fate of their puppies.

"They're going to do their best." Nanny had just spoken to the police.

Roger shook his head. "For what it's worth."

"Do you think they'll find them?" Anita asked anxiously.

"I have my doubts they'll even look," Roger sighed. "In a city of ten million people, fifteen lost puppies doesn't mean much."

Pongo looked over at Perdy. Was she listening? No, she was so grief-stricken she hadn't heard a word. For a moment he, too, stared sightlessly into the fire. Then he slipped through the door and made his way to the roof.

Pongo stood silhouetted against a huge, blue, winter moon. He opened his mouth and barked loudly, then barked again and again. He stopped and scanned the rooftops below. There was no answering sound. He barked again.

Downstairs, Perdy lifted her head at the sound of Pongo's barking. She got up and trotted quietly up the stairs. As she emerged onto the roof, there was Pongo, standing against a deep black sky sprinkled with stars, barking a message over and over.

Suddenly a faraway bark echoed through the night air. Pongo answered: two short barks, a long one, a short one, and a howl. The other dog repeated it, and faintly, in the distance, a third dog took it up. Encouraged, Pongo repeated the signal again and again.

Downstairs, in the master bedroom, Roger jumped out of bed. "Pongo's on the roof!" he cried, dashing towards the stairs. Grabbing a dressing gown, Anita scrambled after him.

"It won't do any good to wake up the neighbourhood," Roger said to Pongo, as he led him across the attic by the collar.

Anita had hold of Perdy. "We know how you feel," she said sympathetically, "but that won't bring your puppies back."

Pongo's barking had already done its work. From Buckingham Palace to the London streets, corgis, scotties, mutts and mongrels passed the signal to each other. Pongo's message travelled out of the city and into the country.

On a rocky hilltop, a border collie listened to the message. His answering bark echoed through the woods.

In a nearby barn, a draft horse named Punch hung his head through the window and listened attentively. Next to him, an old English sheepdog snored on his back in the hay.

Punch turned away from the window and whinnied

loudly. Fogey, the sheepdog, awoke with a jolt. He jumped to his feet and charged into the aisle, barking madly. Punch swung his head towards the window and snorted.

Fogey galloped to the window. As the border collie barked out the message once more, Fogey repeated it, trying to get it exactly right. Punch took up the signal by slamming his hoof over and over on the wooden floor.

In response, cows mooed, pigs oinked, chickens clucked and sheep rose from sleep and headed down a field. A crow swooped from the sky. Rabbits, wood-peckers, and squirrels woke up and scampered towards the barn. And Kipper, the dog who had talked to Wizzer, streaked across the hills towards the sound of Perdy's bark.

When Kipper ran through the barn door, all the animals were gathered in a circle around Fogey. Kipper pantomimed what he knew: he snagged an empty feed sack and wiggled into it, whimpering like the Dalmatian puppies, then walked out of the barn on his hind legs, with the bag in his mouth.

The animals cawed, woofed, whinnied, mooed and oinked to let him know they understood. Then Kipper led Fogey to the top of a nearby hill, and struck a pointer's stance. Fogey peered into the night. There was the abandoned de Vil mansion a few miles away – but its lights were on, and smoke curled darkly from its chimney. The two dogs exchanged glances. With a short bark, Kipper took off towards the mansion to find the puppies.

Fogey galloped back to the farmyard and barked out a message, using a discarded piece of a farm building as a megaphone. On a nearby hilltop, the collie took up the message. "The puppies are at the abandoned de Vil mansion." It passed over the farms, through the suburbs, and into the great city of London.

11

Prime Suspect

Cruella's morning newspaper blared the news: DOGNAPPING! accompanied by a picture of Nanny sitting by the empty puppy basket.

"Dognapping," she sneered. "Can you imagine?"

Another paper lying on her bed had a different caption: FIFTEEN PUPPIES STOLEN. THIEVES FLEE.

"Fifteen puppies stolen. What precious little creatures." Cruella's voice dripped venom. "Anita and her fool."

She glanced at a picture of Roger and Anita. "Such sad faces. Such sorrow." Cruella thrust the paper aside and laughed. Then she picked up her phone and dialled a well-known number.

The phone woke Anita and Roger from a sound sleep. "It's Scotland Yard!" Roger grabbed the receiver. "Hello, Inspector?" He paused. "Who?"

Anita leaned forward anxiously. "What are they

saying? Have they found them?"

Roger shook his head and handed her the phone.

"Hello?" For a moment, Anita didn't recognize the voice at the other end, and when she did, she wasn't glad to hear it. "Cruella?"

"Anita, darling." Lying back against the pillows of her bed, Cruella smiled, then continued smoothly. "I saw the papers. It's a dreadful thing. You must be crushed." She took a long drag from her cigarette. "I know that our parting was unpleasant and that my words were harsh, but at a time like this our differences don't matter. Do they?"

Anita felt herself softening. "I don't suppose so."

"Is she calling to confess?" Roger demanded.

Anita covered the phone and shot him an indignant look. "Roger, please!"

"Don't listen to her," he pleaded.

"Yes," Anita said to Cruella, "We're doing everything we can."

"I spoke to the police. And Scotland Yard. I'm very sorry to say that I wasn't much help. Have they offered any information?"

Anita was silent.

"It's silly to think that anyone would organize a group to steal puppies," Cruella said.

Roger grabbed the phone from Anita. "Where are they?" he yelled into the receiver.

Anita snatched the phone back from her husband.

"What's the matter with you?" she cried.

"Anita?" Cruella's voice came from the dangling receiver.

"I'm sorry, Cruella," Anita apologized. "He's very upset. If there's any news, I'll let you know. Thanks for ringing."

She hung up and turned to Roger. "That was uncalled for. She may be a lot of things but she's not a thief."

"For me, she's the prime suspect."

"She's been investigated by Scotland Yard. What more do you want?"

Roger shook his head and sighed. "I don't know. I'm sorry. I just feel so helpless."

"However helpless we feel, just imagine how Pongo and Perdy feel."

While Anita and Roger were talking, a chihuahua trotted round the corner, sat down in front of their house, and began to bark.

Inside the house, Perdy nudged Pongo awake. The two dogs scrambled to their feet and barked excitedly. The chihuahua howled in response. The two dogs charged for the door. With a quick practised motion, Pongo unlatched it and they ran out.

"Pongo!" Roger leapt from the bed at the familiar sound of the door unlatching. "He opened the door!" He rushed to the window, while Anita hurried after him. "PONGO!" he shouted. "PERDY!"

With stunned looks on their faces, Roger and Anita watched their dogs disappear down the street.

Skinner was at his bench, tanning a hide, when the ancient black phone on his desk began to ring.

"Mr Skinner?" The voice of Cruella de Vil came over the line. "How are you?" She paused for a moment, not expecting him to answer. "Suspicions are mounting," she said. "It's time."

Skinner smiled, and ran his thumb across the blade of a knife.

"Will you be able to do it tonight?" Cruella demanded.

He tapped his yellow-stained finger once on the mouthpiece.

"All of it?"

He tapped again.

"You'll get paid when you deliver the fur." Cruella paused. Her voice turned cold. "Enjoy."

12

Kipper to the Rescue

At the de Vil mansion, Horace and Jasper sat on old ripped chairs, in front of the dying fire. "Stand up a minute there, mate," Jasper said. "Fire's getting a bit dim."

Horace stood up. Quickly, Jasper pulled the chair out from behind him, crossed it into the fire then returned to his own seat.

The chair burst into flames. Without noticing, Horace lowered himself down and crashed to the floor.

Kipper leapt onto a balcony rail, sailed through a broken window in the de Vil mansion, and fell through the rotted cloth of a bed canopy. An enormous cloud of dust billowed around him as he landed on the ancient mattress. He jumped down to the floor and sniffed his way down the hill.

"I'll be honest with you, mate." Horace sat on the

sagging sofa and untied his shoes. "This job is losing its charm. The housing stinks, the food's lousy, the lavatory facilities are appalling, and so far, we ain't been paid so much as a quid."

Jasper sprawled on the other side, trying to avoid the protruding sofa springs. "Aw, stop your crying. It's all over tomorrow night. We gets our boodle and we'll be gone fast as you can say 'dead puppies'."

Horace bent over to take off his shoes. Was there something moving in the shadows? "Jasper? Did we make sure them puppies was locked up?"

"We counted every one of them," Jasper said with a belch.

The room was a mess – like the rest of the mansion. There was broken furniture, splintering walls, rotting carpets and crumbling ceilings. Still trembling, Kipper made his way to a set of closed doors and scratched at them. He wondered if he could get them open. He smelled the puppies somewhere nearby.

From the other side of the door came a little cry. They were there! Kipper looked anxiously around for a way to get to them. With a tiny squeak, a mouse scampered in front of him. Using its tail as a pointer, it showed Kipper the bent grille of a heating vent. Kipper wagged his tail and squeezed through.

He emerged from behind the arm of a torn, filthy sofa in the library. There were Dalmatian puppies everywhere: on chairs, bookshelves, tables, and window sills, under sofas, behind curtains, and in the corners. And there were more than fifteen puppies, many more. There were ninety-nine.

With Kipper leading them, the puppies crept through the grille and out of the library. As the last one emerged, Kipper stepped round the corner. Suddenly, Horace lumbered out of the drawing room and stood in the hall, listening carefully. Kipper and the puppies shrank back into the shadows.

With a suspicious scowl on his face, Horace scanned the lounge and checked the library doors. Then he headed to the bathroom.

The line of puppies continued silently towards the entry. All went well until one of the smallest puppies stumbled and slid into a table. A crystal lamp teetered and then crashed to the floor.

"Horace?" Jasper called.

The puppies raced back across the lounge, and wriggled through the broken heating vent back into the library.

"Horace?" Jasper crossed to the steps and yanked a wooden railing from the rotting staircase. Brandishing it over his head, he marched to the library and threw the doors open.

No one was there – except the puppies, of course.

Horace flipped his magazine to the floor and headed

towards the drawing room. He must have been imagining those noises.

Upstairs, Jasper heard the thud of the magazine. As he stopped to listen, a floor board creaked under his foot.

When he heard the creak of the board, Horace grabbed a wooden railing and took a step forwards. His eyes widened with fear as Jasper's shadow appeared on the wall, and he raised his weapon.

Suddenly the two men leapt into the doorway at the same time, screamed loudly, and whacked each other over the head.

Pongo and Perdy had left London far behind and were crossing a field when the bird swooped over them. It hovered above them, then landed right on Pongo's nose. Pongo's eyes crossed in surprise. The bird pecked him hard on the head, then leaned forward and chattered into his ear.

Pongo and Perdy followed the bird as it led them away from an electric fence to a small opening in the enclosure, just big enough for them to squeeze through.

His temper none the better for the blow on the head, Horace entered the library. The puppies cowered before him. One looked especially forlorn.

"You're hungry, ain'tcha?" Horace grinned

maliciously. "I brung you something to eat."

He pulled out a mousetrap with a piece of cheese resting in the trip plate. With a mean laugh, he set the trap on the floor.

"What're you doing?" Jasper demanded, coming into the room. "I asked you to check on the mutts. Not keep 'em company."

Horace pointed to the trap. "Look."

The puppy sniffed the cheese. Jasper scowled, grabbed Horace by the arm and shoved him through the door.

"It was only a joke," Horace whined, as Jasper kicked the door shut.

"It's a waste of cheese," Jasper retorted and pushed Horace hard.

"Not to worry. It's a bit smelly."

"Pongo and Perdy will turn up," Anita said forlornly to Roger. "Won't they?"

Roger stared at the fire. He didn't know what to say.

"If you ask me, they will." Nanny carried a tray of tea things into the living room. "They just went looking for the puppies."

"They won't find them, Nanny," Anita said. "I know they're gone."

"You can't lose hope, dear," Nanny said gently.

"You know who did this, don't you?" Roger said harshly.

"I know what you're thinking," Anita said. "And you're wrong."

"I don't think so." Roger reached for his tea.

"I, for one, wouldn't be the least surprised." In her emotion, Nanny lifted the tea tray just out of Roger's reach. "I'm sorry, dear," she apologized to Anita, "but I wouldn't put it past her."

Nanny lowered the tray and Roger once more reached for his tea, but again, she held it away. "She has an awful temper."

Anita looked troubled.

"The dogs never cared for her." Nanny sat down in a chair and began to drink Roger's tea. "Dogs have a sixth sense about things like that. They can smell ill intentions."

"Roger!" Anita jumped to her feet. "Where's my portfolio?"

A few minutes later, she was kneeling on the nursery floor, throwing aside large sheets of drawing paper. Suddenly the colour drained from her face. She looked up. "Oh, no. You're right. She stole the puppies. This is why."

Tears streamed down Anita's face as she handed the drawing to Roger. It was the picture of the black spotted coat she had designed for Cruella. "She's going to kill the puppies."

Gleaming knives lay against black satin. Lionel

64

Skinner snapped the case shut and loaded his equipment into the old hearse he used as a car. Everything was there: spanners, stretchers, chemicals, tools. He slammed the back door shut and climbed behind the driver's wheel.

Anita and Roger stood at the door of Cruella's city residence. "Can you tell me where she's gone?" Roger asked.

"I would like to oblige you, sir," the butler answered, "but I'm not at liberty to divulge madam's whereabouts."

Anita stepped forward. "Cruella knows *me*. I worked for her. I'm a designer."

"Many people have worked for the firm," the butler said.

"She's going to do something terrible!" Anita cried in desperation. "Can't you help us?"

The butler stared coldly at them. "I'm very sorry. Good evening."

"Will you give her a message?" Roger asked. "Tell her . . ."

The butler shut the door in his face.

". . . tell her we know all about her!" Roger yelled. "We're going to the police!"

13

A Narrow Escape

A t the de Vil mansion, the animals were busy. One squirrel gnawed on a wire in Horace and Jasper's truck, another poked its head out of a heating vent, while a third rolled a walnut into the exhaust.

A few miles away, Pongo and Perdy slowed to a stop, uncertain of which way to go. A border collie barked out a direction. They took off after him.

Jasper stretched and groaned. "I think it's time to let the little yappers have it."

"We ain't supposed to do it," Horace whined. "That's Skinner's job."

"Why should that little runt have all the fun?" Horace grinned. "Howdja wanna do it?"

Crossing over to the fireplace, Jasper picked up a poker. "I personally favour the fire iron."

"How's about I shoot my share?" Horace offered.

"You'll spoil the fur, you idiot. And besides . . ." He pulled up his shirt to reveal a pistol stuck in his waistband. "You're not to be trusted with firearms."

"Two excellent points." Horace kicked over a table and a leg broke off.

Just then, someone knocked at the door. The two men exchanged puzzled looks. "Must be the missus," Jasper said. "Fix your shirt and your hair."

Jasper and Horace smiled broadly, then swung the door open. Their smiles faded. "Hello? Anyone there?" Jasper called.

Behind him, Kipper led the puppies out of the library once again. They slipped around the corner and started up the stairs. Wizzer was the last in line. But neither he nor Kipper had noticed one more puppy, sound asleep behind the library door.

The two thugs slammed the front door. The knocking began again. They whipped it open. No one was there. Jasper and Horace stepped out on the porch, shining their torches into the bushes.

As the puppies made their escape, a woodpecker quietly flew away into the snowy night.

Kipper kept his eye on the line of puppies hurrying up the stairs. Just a few more . . .

The front door banged shut. "Maybe we was hearing things," Horace said loudly in the doorway.

Kipper's heart pounded. If they came in now, all hope was gone.

Just then, the van horn honked loudly. Horace and

Jasper ran outside. Three raccoons were sitting in the front seat.

"GET OUTTA THERE!" Jason screamed.

The raccoons hurried away, their job done. They had given the puppies a few more minutes of precious escape time.

As Wizzer rounded the corner, he saw the magazine that Horace had dropped. Cruella's picture was on the front cover. It was too tempting. Wizzer lifted his leg over the picture of Cruella . . .

Then the front door slammed. "I don't believe me eyes!" Jasper's torch picked out Wizzer scrambling up the stairs, and then the puppies gathered on the landing above. Suddenly Kipper dashed down, grabbed Wizzer by the scruff of the neck and charged up the stairs with him.

The two thugs ran after them. "Drop that puppy, you lousy. . ."

Just then they hit Wizzer's wet patch, skidded over the magazine, and crashed to the floor.

The puppies stampeded through the upstairs hall.

Horace and Jasper rose slowly to their feet and marched up the stairs.

"I don't care what you say, I think we'd better be careful," Horace growled.

"You're afraid of puppies now?" Jasper sneered.

"It ain't about being afraid. It's about being careful."

"Careful of what?" Jasper said scornfully.

At that moment, their feet hit a missing tread on the staircase. The carpet runner yanked forward, and, as they watched in horror, pulled a large cabinet towards the edge of the staircase. It stopped and swayed threateningly above them.

Suddenly Horace and Jasper crashed through the stairs. The cabinet's upper doors swung open, spilling a hundred paperweights down on them.

In a crockery cupboard, beneath the stairs, Horace and Jasper stood waist-deep in broken jars and paperweights. "Good thing that cabinet didn't fall on us," Horace muttered.

The cabinet teetered delicately on the edge of the stairs. Wizzer gave it a small push with his nose and it toppled forwards, crashed onto the stairs, and slid half-way down, covering the gaping hole that Horace and Jasper had made. The two men turned on their torches just as the lower doors burst open, dumping forks, spoons and knives over their heads.

As the puppies made their way to the top of the mansion, Jasper and Horace fought their way out of the crockery cupboard.

"I ain't trying them stairs again." Horace brushed a few pieces of broken china from his hair.

"If you ain't going up the stairs, how do you

propose to collect the mutts? Sprout wings and fly?"
Jasper snarled.

"No. I'm going to ride up in a nice lift." He crossed
to an iron and glass door and opened it. "Didn't know
we had one of these, did you?"

"You tried it?"

"I haven't, but I'm sure it's going to be a very
pleasant ride indeed." He sounded smug. It wasn't
often that Horace got the best of Jasper. Jasper
scowled and stepped inside.

Horace slammed the door, and the lights went on.

The gears whirred, the car rose. Then the single
rusty cable that held the lift snapped, and the car
hurtled down. There was a terrible crash, and the
cable spooled noisily down on top of the lift car. The
glass and iron door fell open onto the basement floor.

Horace and Jasper were a mess. Their trousers had
fallen to their ankles, their hats were scrunched down
over their ears. Jasper's shoe was stuck to the lift floor.
It lifted free with a peeling noise.

Kipper nosed open a service door and led the
puppies on to the roof. Peering over the edge, he saw
Fogey down below in the service court and barked out
a greeting.

One of the puppies slid down the roof and landed in
the broad gutter below. One by one, the others
followed him. But Wizzer turned and went back into
the house. He had something to do before he left.

"It's your great bulk that caused that last calamity," Jasper snarled at Horace.

Horace scowled. "I ain't taking any more lip."

"Stop your whining." Jasper shoved him hard. "We have ninety-nine stinking dogs to find and kill."

Wizzer sat very still in the hall. A slow grin spread across Jasper's face when he saw him. "Come here, you speckled lap rat," he crooned nastily.

The puppy didn't move. Jasper raced towards him, and when he saw the hole, it was too late to stop. He fell straight down and landed on a billiard table, which collapsed under his weight. Jasper stared into the face of a stuffed water buffalo directly above him. With a creak, it dropped on top of him, pinning him to the table.

Horace ran through a bedroom, missed the hole that Jasper had just fallen through, and flashed his light up and down the hall. There was Wizzer, racing for the linen cupboard. Horace rushed after him. He'd get that puppy now. It couldn't escape.

But the room was empty. There was nothing but snow, ice, tar stains and a gaping broken wall with a long drop to the ground.

"Where've you gone, you little rat?" Horace cursed.

Wizzer forced himself to lie on his belly so he would blend in with the snow and the tar stains. The torch passed over him; Horace did not see him.

One by one, the puppies slid down the copper spout and rolled into the snow, where Fogey shepherded them into the woods. On the roof, Kipper placed the last puppy in the gutter. He looked round, then barked. Wizzer was missing. Kipper charged across the attic to the stairs.

Wizzer looked out the hole in the wall. It was a very long drop to the ground from here, and it didn't look like a soft landing. Below him was the hard frozen ice of a duck pond. Wizzer turned and looked in the other direction. There was Horace and his torch.

Suddenly Kipper appeared in the doorway. He growled angrily at Wizzer, and motioned him up the attic stairs.

Wizzer trotted across to him. But he couldn't resist one last fierce bark at Horace's retreating back.

Horace spun round and trained his torch in the direction of the bark. The beam lit up Wizzer's tail wagging defiantly at the bottom of the stairs.

In a rage, Horace rushed after him. He hit the ice on the linen room floor, skidded across the room, and sailed through the hole in the wall.

Wizzer barked triumphantly, then charged up the stairs.

Down below, a beam of light flashed wildly across the duck pond, followed by a long scream. Horace crashed through the ice, and sank to the bottom of the pond.

14

Reunited

Feeling very pleased with herself, Cruella drove through the deep snow of the countryside in her Panther de Vil. She was driving recklessly, but she didn't care. Danger exhilarated her. She blasted her horn and sped through a village. The moment she had been waiting for had almost arrived.

Kipper watched Wizzer slide down the copper pipe to safety. With a sigh of relief, he turned towards the roof door.

There stood a battered, dusty, bruised Jasper, with a fireplace poker held high over his head. "It's time to pay the piper," he snarled.

Kipper dodged as Jasper swung at him again and again. Suddenly he lunged and clamped his teeth on Jasper's hand.

With a howl, Jasper dropped the poker. Kipper bared his teeth and growled furiously.

Jasper pushed his coat aside and yanked out his

73

pistol. "I'm very sorry," he hissed, "but I'm going to have to bid you adieu."

Terrified, Kipper backed to the edge of the roof. His back paws scraped against the tar, then slipped. He hung by his front paws for a moment, then fell to the ground.

Jasper looked down at Kipper's limp body and laughed. "Stupid mutt. . ." He scratched his head with the barrel of his pistol. ". . . gun ain't even loaded."

The pistol discharged, blowing Jasper's hat and toupée off his head.

Just then, Cruella's Panther de Vil came to a screeching halt in front of the mansion. Jasper froze in panic. "The Missus! HORACE!" he bawled.

As Cruella stepped out of her car, he saluted her from the roof. "Evening, ma'am," he said smoothly.

She looked up angrily. "What are you doing up there?"

As Cruella impatiently tapped her left foot, a skunk waddled out of the bushes and wiggled into the driver's seat of her car and sat down right next to her black-and-white fur handbag.

Jasper was silent.

"ANSWER ME!!" she shrieked.

"I was fetching the puppies, ma'am," he stuttered in terror.

Cruella's eyes narrowed. "And where *are* the

74

puppies?" she demanded furiously.

Jasper shifted from one foot to the other. "I'm not entirely certain. I'd have to check with my associate. Horace?"

A few yards away, a frozen Horace tried to crawl out of the pond. He was covered in ice from the tip of his nose to his feet.

Jasper cupped his hands around his mouth. "HORACE!"

With a crunch of breaking ice, Horace rose to his feet.

Cruella shook her fist at Jasper. "Get down from there and catch those puppies!" There was a threat in her voice, which she meant to carry out, if she didn't see those puppies soon.

The policeman came out of Cruella de Vil's London residence carrying the pelt of the slaughtered tiger from London Zoo.

On the pavement, Anita turned pale. Roger put a protective arm around her.

"Your suspicions were justified," the Captain said, gesturing to the skin. "According to the staff, Ms de Vil left early in the day for family property in Suffolk. Officers will be on the lookout for your puppies and Ms de Vil." He paused, then said grimly, "I hope we're not too late."

★ ★ ★

Fogey watched over his flock, resting in the deep snow that covered the sheep meadow.

A short distance away, Cruella's Panther de Vil pulled up by the side of the road. She gazed suspiciously at the puppy tracks that seemed to lead straight to the sheep. Something was wrong here. Still, there was no sign of the puppies. Cruella rolled up her window and drove the car away.

As the car rolled out of sight, the sheep rose to their feet. Ninety-eight puppies tumbled out from beneath them. Fogey barked an order and they continued on their trek.

At the de Vil mansion, a trembling cold Horace, encrusted with icicles, climbed into the truck.

"You just had to let them puppies slip away, didn't you?" said a furious Jasper. "Never paying attention!"

"Where was *you*?" Horace sulked.

"I wasn't splashing about in a pond! If we don't get them puppies back, it's quite literally our heads." He turned the key over and over in the starter. The engine spluttered feebly. "Go out and check the tailpipe," he ordered. "I think we got a condensation problem."

"One of these days, I'm gonna be full up of you!" Horace muttered. He waddled to the back of the truck. "WHAT'S IT I'M LOOKING FOR?"

76

"MOISTURE IN THE EXHAUST!" Jasper screamed.

With a sullen nod, Horace crouched in front of the exhaust. Jasper floored the gas pedal. The engine fired. The walnut that the squirrel had shoved in the exhaust exploded out like a shot and blasted Horace.

At the farm, the crow greeted a weary and cold Perdy and Pongo with a loud caw. The horse Punch poked his head out and whinnied a welcome. The two dogs squeezed in through a hole in the side of the barn and rushed down the aisle, looking for their puppies.

A cow mooed. Perdy peered into her stall. There were her puppies! At the sight of their mother, they swarmed out, yelping excitedly.

More puppies peeped shyly out from the other stalls. Perdy and Pongo exchanged a puzzled glance. Where had they all come from? Looking at his mother, Wizzer barked three times, whined twice, and howled.

Perdy and Pongo barked a welcome to the other puppies, who eagerly spilled out of the stalls to join the family. Ninety eight Dalmatians rejoiced at their narrow escape from Cruella de Vil.

Back at the mansion, one small puppy rose on his back

paws to look out of a window, and whimpered sadly. He had been asleep when the others left. Now he was alone and lost and afraid. He wondered if he would ever find them.

Cruella leaned out of her car and gazed at a set of tracks leading to the farm. She smiled and took a drag on her cigarette. The puppies were nearby. This time, they wouldn't get away.

Carelessly, she flicked her ash on the passenger seat. The skunk, who had crawled in the car and lay camouflaged next to her black and white fur handbag, looked up indignantly.

In the barn, Pongo and Fogey conversed in barks, woofs and growls, while Perdy watched over the tired pups.

Pongo and Fogey peered out of a hole in the barn wall. Fogey grumbled. Something was very wrong; he could smell the danger in the air.

Jasper and Horace's truck lurched along the road. The lights flashed on and off, while Jasper pounded the wheel in a fury.

"Turn on the heat, will ya?" Horace hadn't been able to warm up since falling into the frozen pond.

"Not with this thing acting like it is. I don't want to risk losing power."

"Well, I can't stand the cold no more! I want

HEAT!" Horace flipped a switch. Flames shot out from the heating vents. The men screamed as the cab turned into an inferno. The truck swerved into a snowbank, its doors flew open, and the two men leapt out.

Outside the barn where the Dalmatians were hiding, Cruella's car rolled to a silent stop.

Fogey barked an alert, and Pongo and Perdy scrambled out from the stalls, with the puppies following.

"This is extraordinary," Cruella spat out, as she picked her way through the mud. "I have to tramp through the mud and muck because those morons can't keep track of a bunch of infant dogs."

At the sound of her voice, Pongo and Perdy herded the puppies down the aisle. Punch stood ready to defend the doors.

Cruella stopped, pulled out a tissue and wiped a spot of mud from her shoe. As she straightened up, the crow sailed out of the barn window, swooped over her head, and snatched her fur hat.

Cruella screamed and stamped her feet. "JASPER! HORACE!" Where were those fools when she needed them?

Their faces black with soot, Jasper and Horace picked themselves up.

"We'd better have that heater adjusted," Horace grumbled.

Jason shot him a menacing look. "What did I say about the heat? WHAT DID I SAY?"

"I don't want you yelling at me right now," Horace muttered.

"Because you know you done wrong?" his partner demanded.

"No."

"Because you know you're the stupidest toe rag the European Community's ever gonna produce?"

"No," Horace said stubbornly.

Jasper grabbed him by the throat. "Then tell me why you don't think I oughta yell at you right now?"

"We ain't got the time."

"Oh? Why not?"

"Because the van's gonna blow up."

An ominous hissing came from the van. The two men looked at each other, then hurled themselves off the road as it exploded into a ball of fire.

Cruella peered through a knothole in the barn doors. There was nothing to see, but the back of a horse.

Suddenly, the horse whinnied and his hooves slammed into the doors. They burst open, sending Cruella flying across the yard and into the muck.

Horace and Jasper rose to their knees to survey the damage. Their van was a wreck. Nothing was left but a twisted frame and burning tyres.

"My van's gone," Jasper whimpered in shock.

"Reduced to a burning hulk."

"When are you going to listen to me?" Horace whined. "It's the animals! They've done this to us."

"I don't want to hear no more of that twaddle!" Jasper snarled. "If this is the work of dumb animals, then I'll clasp me hands together, turn me eyes to the heavens, and beg that I'm struck senseless by our dear . . ."

His voice died out. Hurtling down from the skies, straight at his head, was the grille of the truck. Thinking quickly, Jasper grabbed Horace and thrust him directly underneath it.

15
All 101

L ionel Skinner walked slowly up the broken steps of the de Vil mansion. As he entered, he bowed and tipped his hat to the puppy in a mock greeting.

The puppy who had been left behind greeted him with a happy yelp. Then he realized his mistake. This man had not come to rescue him. In terror, he backed away.

With a gloved hand, Skinner reached for the puppy.

Suddenly he heard a growl behind him. A bruised and battered Kipper limped forward, his teeth bared menacingly.

As Skinner stared, the dog charged. Skinner opened his mouth in a silent scream as Kipper's jaws closed around his ankle.

Kipper charged again. Skinner fell to the floor, clutching both ankles in agony.

With the puppy in tow, Kipper hobbled to the floor.

★ ★ ★

Puppies streamed silently through the hole in the side of the barn, as Cruella walked through the barn doors. "Now listen to me, you country bumpkins – you obviously have no idea what you are mucking about with. You know what I'm here for. The puppies! If you don't hand them over to me immediately, I will simply rip your sorry heads from your bodies and personally sauté, soufflé, skewer and skin your squealing carcasses into shish-kebabs and hand luggage."

A flock of chickens had gathered on the beam above her.

Cruella smiled and looked up. The puppies, at last.

Instead, a shower of eggs dropped from the rafters, drenching her clothes and dribbling down her face and shoulders.

Cruella cleared her throat. She would give them one more chance. "I have an announcement to make."

A final egg plopped on her head.

"Look! Tracks!" Horace cried.

Jasper grinned in triumph. "If dogs were so smart, they'd know not to leave tracks for wary predators. Such as us."

The two men began to follow the tracks.

Over the hill, a horde of rabbits hopped towards an

electric fence, leaving a puppy-like trail.

As Horace and Jasper approached the electric fence, the rabbits jumped over it and disappeared into the snow.

Cruella was losing patience. She rammed a pitchfork into a pile of straw. "I know you're in here!" she said furiously.

A wagging tail in the hayloft just above caught her eye. Setting the pitchfork aside, she reached up with both hands and yanked. "I GOT YOU!" she cried.

A plump pink pig toppled over and pinned Cruella to the floor of the barn.

Horace and Jasper dragged a log over to the electric fence.

"You haven't got natural wits," Jasper scolded him. "That's your problem. You would have grabbed hold of that fence, given yourself a nasty jolt, and cooked your tongue before ever thinking it was electrified."

He spat on the wire. It sizzled and popped.

"Point well taken," Horace said, "but what's the log for?"

Jason spoke slowly and distinctly. "We stand on it and hop over the fence, avoiding painful, electric shock."

"Sounds like a plan," Horace agreed.

The two men stepped onto the log. "Raise the leg," Jasper ordered. "Swing 'er out. And push off with the other."

They bent their knees. Horace began to tip and lean away from the fence. Jasper leaned with him.

"Careful!" Horace cried.

"Look out!" Jasper yelled. The log rolled towards the fence. "JUMP!"

The log rolled under the bottom wire, and Jasper and Horace were left only halfway over the electric fence. Horace wobbled wildly, then fell on his bottom. Wires buzzed; sparks flew. Blue electricity lit up crazily around him.

Jasper's mouth flew open and his hat and toupée exploded in the air.

The two men vaulted into the air, then landed heavily in the snow, their limbs vibrating with an electrical charge. They still crackled and buzzed with electricity as they got up and disappeared into the woods.

"Useless, disgusting animals," Cruella snarled. She climbed to the hayloft. She wouldn't give up; no, never. But what was that in the distance? A line of Dalmatians, heading for town.

They had got away. In spite of her best efforts, they had escaped. She stumbled towards the stairs, then stopped suddenly. A raccoon was holding her fur hat.

"Darling, red is not your colour," she said.

As she made her way towards the animal, two other raccoons released a trap door, Cruella fell through the open floor to the cellar. "Whoa!" She landed in a vat of thick, gooey treacle, and with a giant sucking sound, disappeared under the surface. A few seconds later she emerged, glazed with treacle, and sticking to the side of the vat as she tried to climb out.

When she finally stood up, treacle stretched like wires, in long, rubbery strands from her body to the vat.

Still twitching and shaking, Horace and Jasper emerged from the woods. "Thank heavens!" Jasper cried fervently.

"We're saved!" Horace echoed.

Police cars and a police van lined the road. As Jasper and Horace were escorted inside, they smiled happily.

"This looks lovely," said Horace.

"Nice and warm," Jasper agreed.

"No animals, neither," Horace pronounced.

They sat down on the bench seat.

"Thanks, mates," Horace said to the policemen.

Jasper smiled at them. "Much obliged."

The police van doors closed. Only then did Jasper and Horace see their fellow occupant. The top of his hat was chewed away. His pants were torn.

Lionel Skinner's lip was bloody, and his wounded, throbbing ankles were wrapped in handkerchiefs.

Cruella cursed as she ascended from the barn cellar. She was covered in treacle. With every step, her shoes made a sloppy, sucking noise. She wiped her face with the back of her hand. Her eyes were rabid, her lips curled back in a ferocious snarl.

She marched forwards and planted her soggy feet on the floor of the barn. "You beasts, you've won the battle but I'm about to win the wardrobe," she said furiously to the animals. "My spotty puppy coat is in plain sight and leaving tracks. In a few moments I shall have what I came for while you will end up as sausage meat!" she concluded.

In his stall, Punch suddenly reared up on his hind legs, and battered his hooves on the floorboard where Cruella stood. It loosened, flew up, and sent her vaulting into the air.

She arched over the loft, shattered the window and landed in a dung heap, which erupted with squealing pigs.

Police cars surrounded the Panther de Vil. A police officer stepped forward and shone his torch into the dung heap. "Ms de Vil?"

Cruella's head emerged from the muck. "Yes?"

The officer tried not to smile. "We have a warrant for your arrest."

The farmyard animals erupted into a jubilant chorus of whinnies, caws, cackles and oinks.

Lights flashed, sirens wailed and radios barked out commands in a small village nearby. The police officers had found Pongo, Perdy and the puppies.

"I make it ninety-eight pups," an officer said into a radio. "The two adults makes it one hundred even."

Perdy rose and barked sharply. Kipper was limping up the main road, carrying a puppy by the scruff of his neck.

"Make that one hundred and one Dalmatians, sir!" the officer corrected.

A line of police cars pulled out of the village. Pongo, Perdy and their puppies rode in the back seat of one car. With his paw, Perdy pressed down on the electric window button. Then he stuck his head through the window and barked joyfully.

Fogey's deep bark answered, and carried the message. From the surrounding hills echoed barks, moos, squeals, whinnies and cackles.

In the police van, an enraged Cruella sat next to Mr Skinner. "I've never met more incompetent fools than you three."

She reached into her coat pocket and took out a soggy pack of cigarettes. Angrily, she threw them on the floor. "My business, my reputation, my life have

88

been ruined because you fools got outsmarted by a pack of puppies. . ."

She reached for her black and white purse, but picked up the skunk instead. "You call yourselves men. Ha!"

Still not noticing what she was doing, Cruella grabbed the skunk's tail as if it were a purse flap. "You're no better than the dumb animals who got the better of you," she sneered.

She glanced down, looking for a new pack of cigarettes. The skunk fixed her with a clear-eyed stare. Her mouth dropped open. Mr Skinner, Jasper and Horace gasped.

The skunk expelled its foul-smelling musk all over Cruella.

16

One Big Happy Family

"They're here! Hurry!" Nanny cried at the living room window.

Roger and Anita hurried out. Pongo, Perdy and the puppies hopped out from the police car and scrambled towards them.

"Pongo, old boy! Perdy!" Roger cried joyfully.

"The puppies!" Anita cried, her arms held open to receive them.

"The puppies, indeed!" Nanny echoed.

Roger turned to the policemen. "Thank you, gentlemen. We'll be forever grateful."

The policemen tipped their hats, got into their car and pulled away. As Roger and Anita began to herd the puppies into the house, another police car pulled up.

Roger and Anita exchanged puzzled glances. Nanny tapped Roger on the shoulder and pointed down the street.

A line of police cars extended around the corner.

Out of each car scrambled dozens of yelping Dalmatian puppies.

"We can't. We don't have room," Anita said. "Roger, please."

Roger was smiling. "We'll work something out. We'll get a bigger place."

Pongo barked his agreement.

"We have seventeen as it is," Nanny added. "What's a few more?"

Perdy looked at Anita pleadingly. Anita frowned. "You'll have dozens of children, you know."

Perdy nodded.

Anita continued in a warning voice. "I won't have them chewing up the carpets and barking at all hours of the night."

Perdy shook her head.

Anita looked to Roger, who pointed to the bottom of the stairs, where eighty-four puppies waited eagerly for her decision.

Anita sighed, then smiled. "Everybody inside. Breakfast is getting cold," she said.

As the puppies scrambled into the house, Roger picked up the newspaper. There was Cruella on the front page, her hair coated with treacle and dung, her clothes torn and filthy.

A slow smile spread across his face. He had a wonderful idea; one that would end all their problems.

91

Anita and Roger sat anxiously on the sofa in the video game company office, watching Herbert play Roger's new game, while Allan hovered nearby.

The little Dalmatian hopped across a river and zoomed down a ravine, as Herbert played with maniacal concentration.

Roger nudged Anita and pointed to the screen. Suddenly, Cruella's face came onscreen. Her laughter echoed hideously.

Anita gasped. Outside, waiting on the terrace with the other puppies, Wizzer's ears shot up in surprise.

"Cool," said Herbert, approvingly.

Squealing and yipping in fear the puppies on the terrace fled.

Allan glanced at Herbert. The kid nodded, hopped down from his chair and picked up his bookbag. "Get out your chequebook," he ordered. He looked over at Roger. "Excellent villain, mate."

"Congratulations," Allan said. "Let's go to my office."

As they left for Allan's office, Wizzer's head popped up in the open window. He trotted over to the television where Cruella's face was frozen on the screen. With his paw, he pressed the joystick. Cruella's image exploded. Wizzer wagged his tail and barked happily.